What Makes This Insect Cool?

by Ms. Raught's class
with Tony Stead

capstone

What Are Insects?

Insects fly, crawl, and sometimes bother us.

But are they creepy?

Read on to find out.

illustrated by Qiyliir

Meet the Insects!

by Makayla and Zoey

Some insects crawl.

Beetles, ladybugs, and centipedes creep on the ground.

Grasshoppers and crickets can jump!

Insects Are All Around

by Bishop

Some insects fly.

Flies, dragonflies, and beetles float in the air.

They are born from eggs.

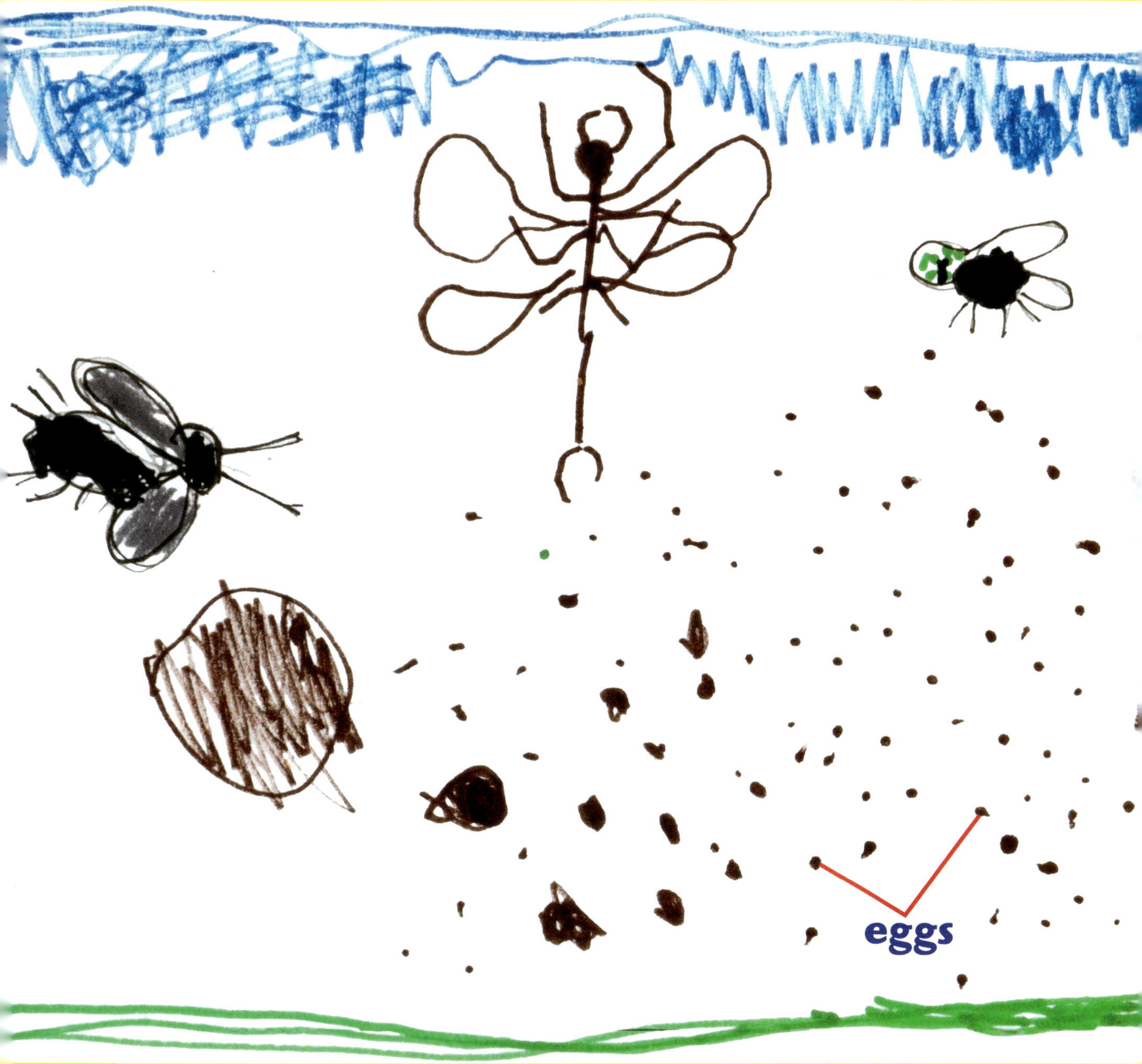
eggs

What Parts Do Insects Have?

by Imani and Julian

Many insects have wings.

These help the insects fly.

wings

Insects have legs.

These help the insects crawl.

Antennae are parts that help the insects feel.

antennae
legs

What Do Insects Eat?

by Asher, Kevin, Renai, Sakhi

Insects eat all kinds of food.

Some insects eat wood and grass.

They use their mouth parts to feed themselves.

Some taste with their feet!

Some insects eat houses, and some insects bite us.

Are insects cool or creepy? You decide!

illustrated by Renai